Thank you to the generous team who gave their time
and talents to make this book possible:

Author
Barbara Oswald

Illustrator
Lori Rorabeck

Creative directors
Caroline Kurtz, Jane Kurtz and Kenny Rasmussen

Translator
Amlaku B. Eshetie

Designer
Beth Crow

Ready Set Go Books, an Open Hearts Big Dreams Project

Special thanks to Ethiopia Reads donors and staff for believing in this project and helping get it started-- and for arranging printing, distribution, and training in Ethiopia.

ISBN: 978-1657648791
Library of Congress Control Number: 2020920678

Republished: 10/25/20

Music of the City

የከተማ ድምጾች

English and Amharic

It is morning.

ጧት ነው።

The city wakes.

ከተማዋ ነቅታለች።

Listen to the sounds it makes.

የምትፈጥረውን ድምጽ አዳምጡ።

Cars rush by.

መኪኖች ይፋጠናሉ።

Engines hum.

ሞተሮቻቸው ይተምማሂሉ።

A train is
rumbling like
a drum.

ባቡሩ እንደከበሮ
ድም-ዳም ይላል።

Heels click
  on the street.

የጫማ ተረከዞች በጎዳና
  ላይ ቅው-ቋ ይላሉ።

Feel the rhythm of
donkey's feet.

ከአህዮች ኮቴ
ድምጽ ጋር
ይመሳሰላል።

Outside a shop, pots clang.

ከሱቆች ደጃፍ
እንሥራዎችና
ጀበናዎች
ያቃጨላሉ።

Something crashes
with a bang.

የሆነ ነገር
"ግው" ብሎ
ተጋጭቶ
ተሰበረ።

Sheep bleat. በጎች ባዓዓ ይላሉ።

Chickens cluck.

ዶሮዎች ያሽካካሉ።

Beep! Beep! Beep! Honks a truck.

ጺጽ! ጺጽ! ጺጽ!
መኪኖች ጡሩምባቸውን ይነፋሉ።

Beep!
Beep!
Beep!

Prayers call out from domes and towers.

ከቤተክርስቲያንና መስጊዶች
የጸሎት ድምጾች ይሰማሉ።

Bees buzz on the flowers.

ንቦች አበቦች ላይ ብዝዝዝ እያሉ
ይቀስማሉ።

Cats meow.
Dogs bark.

ድመቶች ሚያው፤
ውሾች ው ው!

Birds sing in the park.

ወፎች በፓርኩ ውስጥ ይዘምራሉ::

All things have music. Hear it play.

ሁሉም ነገር ሙዚቃዊ ድምጽ
አለው። አዳምጡት።

What will be YOUR song today?

ዛሬ የእናንተ ሙዚቃ ምንድን ነው?

About The Story

Addis Ababa became the capital of Ethiopia in the 1890s, when Menelik II became Emperor of Ethiopia and chose a spot for a city to be named new flower. Building houses would take a lot of wood, so the emperor looked for a fast-growing tree. Australia supplied eucalyptus trees that still grow along city streets and out in the countryside. Now millions of people live in Addis Ababa, the biggest city in Ethiopia and one of the highest capitals anywhere in the world. In recent years, China has invested in building new roads, skyscrapers, and trains that carry at least 300,00 passengers an hour.

About The Author and Illustrator

Barbara Oswald is a lawyer in Madison, Wisconsin. Lori Rorabeck is a language and reading teacher in Milwaukee, Wisconsin. Barbara and Lori are sisters who share a love of reading and an appreciation for the beauty and power of books. They are grateful for the opportunity to collaborate on a book for Open Hearts Big Dreams.

Barbara and Lori

About Ready Set Go Books

Reading has the power to change lives, but many children and adults in Ethiopia cannot read. One reason is that Ethiopia doesn't have enough books in local languages to give people a chance to practice reading. Ready Set Go books wants to close that gap and open a world of ideas and possibilities for kids and their communities.

When you buy a Ready Set Go book, you provide critical funding to create and distribute more books.

Learn more at: http://openheartsbigdreams.org/book-project/

Ready Set Go 10 Books

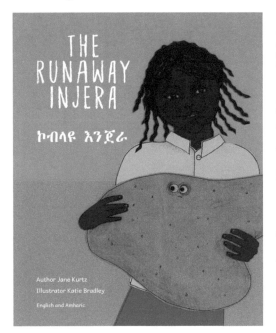

In 2018, Ready Set Go Books decided to experiment by trying a few new books in larger sizes.

Sometimes it was the art that needed a little more room to really shine. Sometimes the story or nonfiction text was a bit more complicated than the short and simple text used in most of our current early reader books.

We called these our "Ready Set Go 10" books as a way to show these ones are bigger and also sometimes have more words on the page. The response has been great so now our Ready Set Go 10 books are a significant number of our titles. We are happy to hear feedback on these new books and on all our books.

About Open Hearts Big Dreams

Open Hearts Big Dreams began as a volunteer organization, led by Ellenore Angelidis in Seattle, Washington, to provide sustainable funding and strategic support to Ethiopia Reads, collaborating with Jane Kurtz. OHBD has now grown to be its own nonprofit organization supporting literacy, innovation, and leadership for young people in Ethiopia.

Ellenore Angelidis comes from a family of teachers who believe education is a human right, and opportunity should not depend on your birthplace. And as the adoptive mother of a little girl who was born in Ethiopia and learned to read in the U.S., as well as an aspiring author, she finds the chance to positively impact literacy hugely compelling!

About the Language

Amharic is a Semetic language -- in fact, the world's second-most widely spoken Semetic language, after Arabic. Starting in the 12th century, it became the Ethiopian language that was used in official transactions and schools and became widely spoken all over Ethiopia. It's written with its own characters, over 260 of them. Eritrea and Ethiopia share this alphabet, and they are the only countries in Africa to develop a writing system centuries ago that is still in use today!

About the Translation

Translation is currently being coordinated by a volunteer, Amlaku Bikss Eshetie who has a BA degree in Foreign Languages & Literature, an MA in Teaching English as a Foreign Language, and PhD courses in Applied Linguistics and Communication, all at Addis Ababa University. He taught English from elementary through university levels and is currently a passionate and experienced English-Amharic translator. As a father of three, he also has a special interest in child literacy and development. He can be reached at: khaabba_ils@protonmail.com

Find more Ready Set Go Books on Amazon.com

 To view all available titles, search "Ready Set Go Ethiopia" or scan QR code

 Chaos

 Talk Talk Turtle

 The Glory of Gondar

 We Can Stop the Lion

 Not Ready!

 Fifty Lemons

Count For Me

 Too Brave

 Tell Me What You Hear

CPSIA information can be obtained
at www.ICGtesting.com
Printed in the USA
LVHW070009040622
720468LV00002B/19